The Princess Gown

by Linda Leopold Strauss

Illustrated by Malene Reynolds Laugesen

⇥ ⇤

HOUGHTON MIFFLIN COMPANY

BOSTON 2008

Text copyright © 2008 by Linda Leopold Strauss
Illustrations copyright © 2008 by Malene Reynolds Laugesen

www.houghtonmifflinbooks.com

The text of this book is set in Garth Graphic.

The illustrations are oil crayon and linseed oil on colored paper.

Library of Congress Cataloging-in-Publication Data

Strauss, Linda Leopold.
The princess gown / written by Linda Leopold Strauss ; illustrated by Malene Reynolds Laugesen.
p. cm.
Summary: If the wedding dress young Hanna's family is making is not chosen for the princess,
they will go to the poorhouse, but thanks to Hanna's sharp eyes and artistic ability, her father
stands a very good chance of becoming Embroiderer to the Princess.
ISBN-13: 978-0-618-86259-7 (hardcover)
ISBN-10: 0-618-86259-5 (hardcover)
[1. Dressmaking—Fiction. 2. Princesses—Fiction. 3. Clothing and dress—Fiction.
4. Embroidery—Fiction.] I. Laugesen, Malene Reynolds, ill. II. Title.
PZ7.S91245Pri 2008
[E]—dc22
2007012923

Manufactured in Singapore

TWP 10 9 8 7 6 5 4 3 2 1

anna scrambled up the tree by the palace and inched out onto the branch overlooking the garden. Yes, there sat the princess on her favorite chair, feeding the small gray squirrel with one ear just slightly larger than the other. How beautiful the princess was! And how tenderly she talked to her little squirrel.

Hanna needed to get home, but first she sent a wish over the wall.

Please, Princess Annabel, she begged silently. *Please choose Papa's.*

Then Hanna raced home.

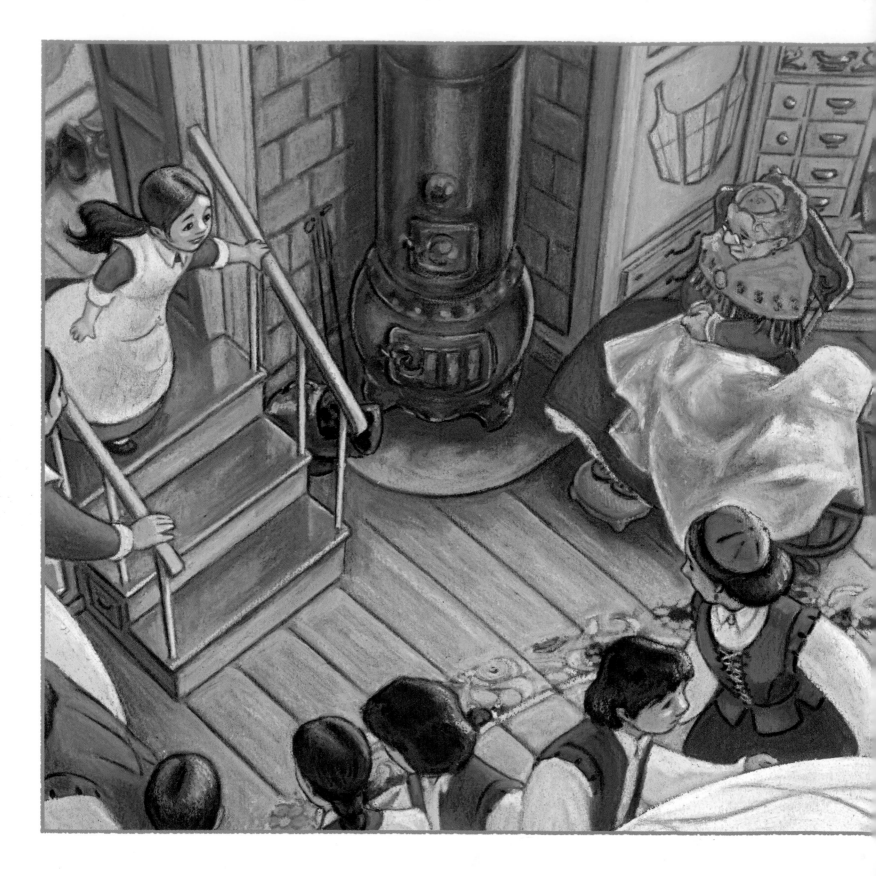

"Stop!" warned Hanna's brothers and sisters as Hanna burst into the workroom.

"I just want to see if Papa's finished," said Hanna.

"So what do you think, my Hanna?" asked Papa as he sewed a pearl to the bodice of the wedding dress. "Will the princess like it?"

Hanna couldn't imagine another dress as beautiful as Papa's. It was a drift of blossoms, a spun-sugar confection, sparkling foam strewn upon the ocean. And soon Papa would wrap it in satin and take it to the palace, where tomorrow morning Princess Annabel would select her wedding gown from the offerings of all the tailors in the kingdom.

"Oh, Papa, she'll love it!" Hanna stepped closer.

"Not a toe over the chalk line, Miss Berry-fingers," Mama said sternly, "until the dress is done."

"Let the child be," Grandma told Mama from her corner by the fire. "She's an artist, like her papa. Look how she's painted this workroom. Look how she's decorated your chalk circle!"

But Mama was worried. Papa had gone perilously into debt to make this dress. If the princess chose Papa's, he'd become Embroiderer to the Princess. But if she chose another, Hanna's beloved family was headed for the poorhouse. (Hanna didn't know what a poorhouse was, but she could tell it wasn't good to go there.) So although her brothers and sisters had all helped sew the dress, Hanna, whose hands were always messy, wasn't allowed to touch it.

"Aahh," breathed Papa. "The last pearl. Almost the last stitch."

"Hurry," warned Mama. "The deadline is sundown!"

"The final stitch," said Papa, "must be Hanna's. This family may never again sew a dress for a princess, and our youngest must be part of it. Hanna, go wash. Rachel will help you."

Rachel scrubbed Hanna from head to toe. "I don't stitch with my *stomach*," Hanna complained, but Rachel kept scrubbing.

When Hanna returned, Papa handed her a threaded needle. She kneeled by the dress, and carefully, as all the Abraham children had been taught practically since the cradle, she crafted a stitch in its hem.

Then she gasped.

She pointed.

A spot. On the smooth silk panel on the skirt's left side. Almost invisible, but a spot nonetheless.

Papa went ashen.

Hanna checked her fingers. She hadn't made that spot! She hadn't!

"Maybe the queen won't notice," said Papa bravely, though everyone said the queen had the eyes of a hawk.

Rachel suggested sponging, but that might leave a ring. Hanna's oldest brother, Joseph, wanted to replace the panel, but Papa had no more silk. Cover the spot with lace? Papa said it would be lumpy.

Hanna studied the spot. What was that shape? Could it be? Grabbing Papa's chalk, she whispered to Grandma, then quickly drew on the floor.

Grandma nodded. "Heat water to warm my fingers," she told Hanna. "Bring me the dress," she told Papa.

The family stared. Papa hesitated.

"And a needle," Grandma told him, "and your finest thread."

Everyone watched Grandma's needle fly through the delicate fabric. First the left panel, then the right. When she had finished, a tiny embroidered squirrel nestled in the folds of the left side of the skirt. On the right . . . an acorn!

"A squirrel!" cried Mama. "On a wedding dress! We're ruined."

"Take the dress to the palace," Grandma told Papa calmly. "We will have a decision by nightfall tomorrow."

Everyone went to bed early. At first light, Papa opened the door, and Hanna slipped her hand silently into his. The king had invited the townspeople to be present for the selection of the gowns, and Hanna had no intention of being left behind.

A crowd had already gathered around the silk-draped stand in the center of the palace courtyard. Papa lifted Hanna onto his shoulders, and she gasped: There on the stand, arranged on forty velvet dressmaker's forms, were forty exquisite wedding dresses. Three of the dresses stood on a golden platform. And one of them was Papa's!

A trumpet sounded. Slowly the royal family entered the courtyard and mounted the stand, followed by a train of courtiers and ladies-in-waiting.

"This one's my favorite," the princess said immediately, pointing to Papa's gown, and Hanna's heart started pounding.

The queen, however, inspected the dresses as if they were Arabian horses for purchase. It didn't take her long to find the squirrel. "Do they think we're mad?" she demanded haughtily. "Do they think we're blind? A squirrel on a wedding dress?"

"But I like the squirrel," said Princess Annabel. "It's just like *my* squirrel. See, Mama — one ear is bigger than the other."

"Ridiculous," thundered the queen. "They must be covering mistakes! Who knows what else is wrong with this dress?"

"And look on this side, Mama!" exclaimed the princess. "There's even an acorn for him to eat."

"Preposterous!" said the queen, and she marched to the next gown.

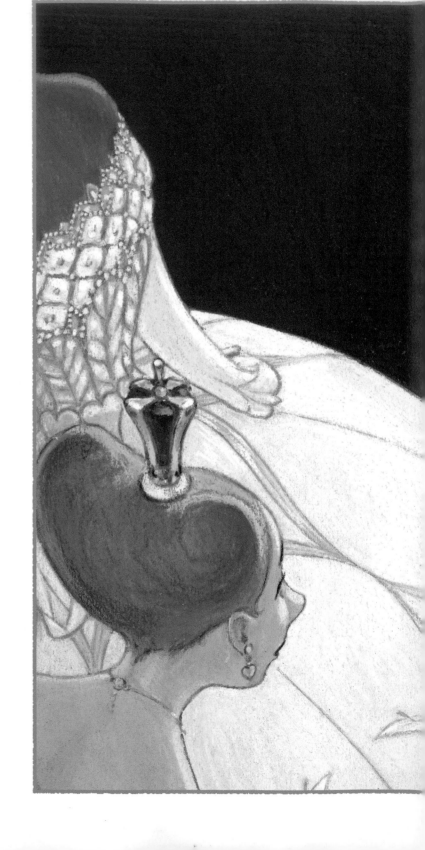

"How curious," one lady-in-waiting said thoughtfully. "Could they have made mistakes on both sides? In exactly the same place?"

"I suppose it's possible," said another. "But look at the artistry of the needlework. The delicacy!"

"Which house created this?" a third lady-in-waiting asked, approaching to examine the gown.

"The House of Abraham. On St. Mary's Road. Haven't I heard . . . ?"

"Yes, always these small surprises. A bird, an acorn, a rose," said the second lady. She stole a glance at the queen to be sure she was listening. "They say it's the latest thing."

"So clever," said the third lady. "So . . . distinctive. And this one . . . so perfect for the princess."

"Ah," sighed the first lady-in-waiting. "It was meant to be."

The queen came slowly back to peer through her lorgnette.

She studied the squirrel.

She studied her daughter.

She turned to her ladies.

"But of course," she said. "A surprise on each garment. How original! A way to mark their work. How delightful!"

"How utterly irresistible!" chorused the ladies-in-waiting.

"Does that mean we can choose the squirrel dress?" the princess asked her mother.

Hanna watched as each lady-in-waiting pressed her hands to her heart. The queen murmured something, and then Princess Annabel's face lit up.

"I think the queen said yes," Hanna told Papa joyfully.

"Yes?" breathed Papa.

"Hooray for the House of Abraham!" the crowd began shouting.

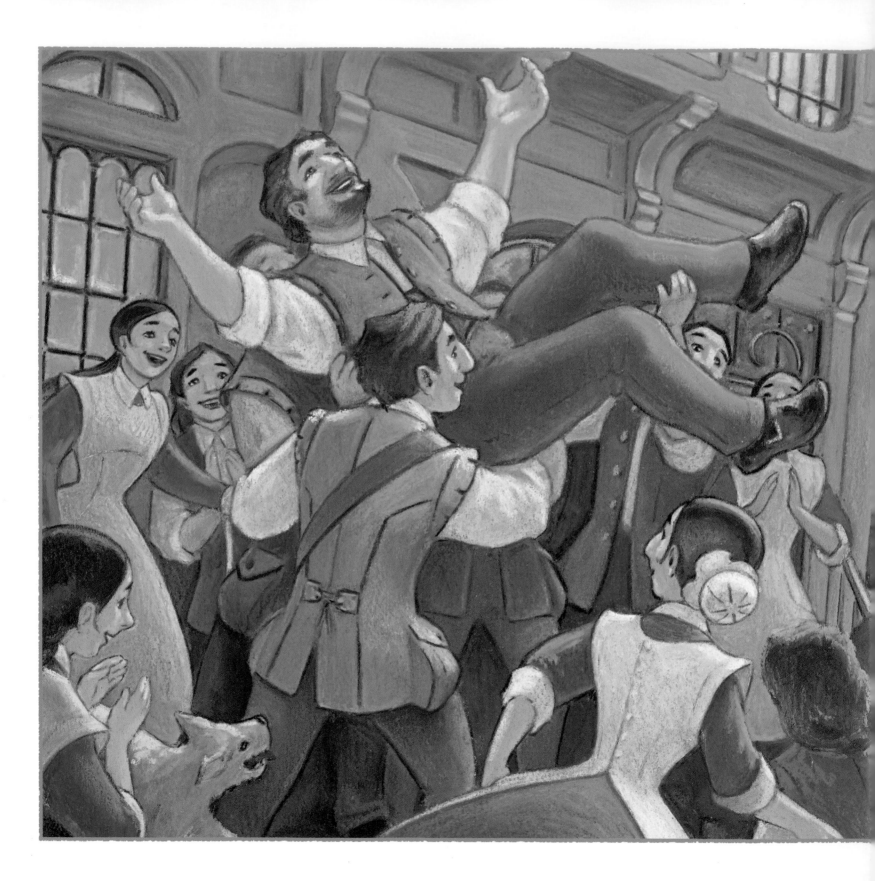

Oh, how the family celebrated! Hanna's sisters showered Papa with kisses, and Hanna's brothers hoisted him to their shoulders. The neighbors led a parade around the block. Grandma and Mama couldn't stop beaming.

"The princess will need many gowns. We will have to work hard," said Mama after the neighbors had left and the family was sitting at supper.

"All those small surprises to think up," said Papa, smiling at Hanna. "But work is for tomorrow. Come see what the queen has sent from the palace." And, taking Hanna's hand, he led the family outside to St. Mary's Road, where a new sign hung over the workshop entrance. *Victor Abraham and Family,* it said proudly. *Embroiderers to the Princess.* And in one corner of the sign was an acorn; in the corner opposite, a small squirrel with one ear just slightly larger than the other.

One year later, at the palace

The End